Smilin' Sam's Corn Maze

Stephanie Scissom

Stephanie Scissom

Smilin' Sam's Corn Maze

LOCAL GIRL, AGE 7, ABDUCTED FROM CORN MAZE ON HALLOWEEN NIGHT. THIRTY-FIVE YEARS LATER, ELIZABETH BRYANT IS STILL MISSING.

That's the headline of the yellowed article I clipped from the Grundy County Herald and eventually taped to the inside cover of this journal, though the clipping is dated. Next October will be forty years since Lizzy was stolen from us.

Lizzy remains missing, a cold case growing colder by the year. I'm not sure anyone still cares about its resolution except for me, her father and her brothers. The wreckage of a family left behind.

According to my doctor, I likely won't live to see that awful anniversary roll around. If I do, I will be lost inside my own mind by then. I accepted the diagnosis of Creutzfeldt-

Jakob Disease stoically. At 71, the thought of death doesn't scare me. But this week, something's changed. Something's happening that makes me want to hold on, for just a little bit longer. I know it sounds crazy, but, for the first time in decades, I might have new information about Lizzy.

My thoughts are scattered now, chaotic. Violent, intense, and dark, then dispersing into nothing, like a murmuration of starlings in a clear, blue sky. I'm writing this down because I can't trust myself to remember. Whatever is happening to me is terrible and beautiful and staggering and I don't know if it's real, a side effect of the medication, or if it's just this horrible disease that's eating my brain. All I know is that it *feels* real. It feels like a chance.

Dr. Hall said the medication might cause vivid dreams. But I haven't told him how vivid they are. How intense and heartbreaking. Seeing Bobby and the boys young and happy again takes my breath away. Seeing *her* again, hearing her innocent giggle, and seeing that gap-toothed smile ... well, it shatters me. I don't want to tell Dr. Hall because I'm afraid he will change my medication, and I want this. I want this so badly. I *need* it. Surely there's a reason this is happening to me because it's not 'dreams.' It's just one dream. Every night when I close my eyes, I find myself back in 1984 on that brutal night when I lost everything. Maybe I can see something I missed before. Maybe I can get her back.

I know it sounds crazy. Perhaps this disease is already raging through my brain like wildfire, but I don't think I'm delusional. Not yet. I know Lizzy is dead. I knew it when they showed me that blood-stained trenchcoat and her day-of-the-week Care Bear panties they'd found stuffed in its pocket.

I just want her back. She belongs with us, in that little cemetery in Paynes Cove, where both sets of her grandparents are buried. Where I will be buried.

I want to bring Lizzy home.

THE DREAM always starts the same. I'm a passenger in our old Chevy Caprice station wagon that we'd affectionately nicknamed 'The Beast.' Bobby sits beside me, singing along to *Drive* by The Cars. He's so handsome, so young, with his sparkling blue eyes and dark hair he wears a little too long. He smiles at me and takes one hand off the wheel to squeeze my knee. The twins are arguing in the 'way back' seat and 12-year-old Josh sits in the middle section by himself, wearing his Walkman earphones in an attempt to ignore them. Then a little hand grabs my other leg and I hear a voice that has been gone for so long, but is instantly recognizable.

"Can I have another Tootsie Roll?"

I turn to look into her face. Sky blue eyes, dark hair, freckles ... the spitting image of her father.

The first two nights, I woke at this point, cheeks wet with tears. The next night, I took sleeping pills before bed, hoping to stay asleep longer.

"Can I have another Tootsie Roll?" she asks.

"No, Elizabeth," Bobby says, in a stern tone he never uses

3

with her when he is actually serious. "If you eat that junk, you won't have room for ... cotton candy and caramel apples!"

Lizzy squeals and claps her hands.

"*You're* sitting up with them if they have bellyaches tonight," I tell Bobby.

He dismisses my statement with a wave of his hand. "It's Halloween, Cath, and these kids are Bryants. They have stomachs of steel."

"Uh huh. That's why this one rides up front, so she doesn't puke on her brothers."

But no one pays attention to me anymore, because we're pulling into the parking lot of Smilin' Sam's Corn Maze. A scarecrow leers at us from the billboard, with shiny, black button eyes and a red triangle of a nose on a yellow face. A little crow perches on his shoulder and they grin ferociously. There's something unnerving about those smiles. Something ... predatory. I feel my own smile fade.

WELCOME TO SMILIN' SAM'S CORN MAZE.
5 ACRES OF FAMILY FUN!

Lizzy bounces in her seat. "I wanna do the maze!"

"It's not for babies," Caleb says. "It's not like Papa Tom's field. There are monsters in there."

"Yeah," Corey adds. "You'll be crying."

"Leave your sister alone," Bobby says. "She knows the monsters are just costumes. Matter-of-fact, I bet she and I can beat you two to the finish."

"You're on!" Corey cries.

Bobby parks and leans forward to offer Lizzy a fist bump. "We got this?"

She grins and nods so hard it makes her pigtails bounce.

"I guess you're stuck with me, Josh," I say, and he offers a beleaguered sigh.

Halloween is on a Wednesday that year, so we are all in costume as we spill out of the station wagon, except for our perpetually sullen pre-teen, Josh. The twins are Ghostbusters, complete with proton packs, Lizzy is Punky Brewster, Bobby is my debonair Han Solo and I'm a white-gowned Princess Leia.

We pay our admission and walk through the gates. Bobby steers us to the side, so we can decide what part of the attraction we're visiting first. *D'yer Mak'er* by Led Zeppelin blasts over the speakers strung up on the light poles and Bobby hugs me from behind. He leans down and whispers in my ear, "This song just makes me want to take you home and make another baby. What do you say?"

I laugh and push him away. "I say I've already given you four just like you. I think that's plenty."

Lizzy grabs his leg and he bends down to swoop her up. She squeals and he grabs her cheeks, forcing her to do duck lips.

"But look how cuuuuuuuute!"

She crosses her eyes for added effect.

I laugh. "That one's more like you than any of them."

Josh points at her and says, "Yeah, that one's cute, and I'm cute ... But look at those two."

The twins stand a few feet away, peering at each other like

they're looking into a mirror. They laugh hysterically, with identical globs of green homemade slime hanging from their nostrils.

"Eh, I don't know," Bobby says objectively. "I think they'll grow into those ears."

That gets a snort from Josh and I smile at Bobby. Then, I hear a noise over the music. It takes me a moment to discern where it's coming from and I look up. High above us, something impossible is happening. The cartoon scarecrow from the billboard pulls his head free from the wood with a mighty grunt. I can't move. I can't scream. The wood creaks and groans as he wrenches one arm loose and uses it to free his other. Then he strains to free his feet. My family is laughing and talking, oblivious to what is happening, even when he rips his torso free and leaps to the ground. He makes a *poing poing poing* noise as he bounces all around us. He finally stops, facing me, and offers me the same ferocious grin. When he speaks, his voice is so high-pitched it hurts my ears.

"Hi!" he says. "I'm Smilin' Sam and I'm here to help YOU get your shit together!"

Stunned, I stare at him. No one else acknowledges him.

"Cathi, Kit Kat, Cath-a-rooni," he says patiently. "It's time to quit fantasizing about Bobby and get to work. You're old now! Your ovaries are shriveled up like raisins! There'll be no more babies." He gives a *tsk tsk* of disapproval. "You couldn't even keep up with the ones you had!"

"Go to hell," I whisper.

He pouts, then shakes his finger in my face. "Do you kiss

your grandkids with that mouth? I'm here to help you, silly goose. We don't have much time before all this goes to mush!"

He slams his fist against my head, making a hollow *knock-knock* sound.

Suddenly, I am drowning. Green slime gushes from my nose and mouth, even my ears. I feel the pressure of it behind my eyes. It tastes thick. Metallic.

The scarecrow grins at me as I suffocate.

I JERK awake in my bed, for a moment thinking I really am dying. Liquid pours from my nose. The metallic taste is even stronger. I half-fall out of bed and stagger to my bathroom.

Flipping on the light, my panic spikes even more when I see that I am covered in blood.

A nosebleed, I realize. *Just a nosebleed.*

I clean myself up and change my gown. Thankfully, I didn't bleed all over the bed, but my favorite pillow is ruined. I retrieve another from the spare bedroom and lie back down. I toss and turn for a while, replaying the dream in my head. I'm sure I won't be able to fall asleep again, but I do.

Smilin' Sam and my family wait just where I left them. Stricken, I look at Lizzy, who beams up at her father, then at Sam, who is also watching them.

"She really is a lovely child, Cath. A little DOLL!"

He pulls a Punky Brewster doll from behind his back. It's a tiny, perfect cartoon replica of Lizzy in her Halloween costume. It has a ring and a pull cord in its back and Smilin' Sam yanks on it.

"Mama!" the doll screams in Lizzy's breathless, terrified voice. "Mama, helpppppppp! He's hurting me!"

I stand frozen in horror, my heart thumping wildly in my chest.

Smilin' Sam gives me a stern look. "Time to pay attention to your kid, Catherine. If you'd done that in the first place, we wouldn't be here. Now, let's throw this thing in reverse."

He snaps his fingers and suddenly, everything moves backwards in a dizzying blur. When we stop, we're standing at the ticket booth again. Bobby pockets his change and we step inside the gate.

Smilin' Sam jumps out of the shadows, startling me. I am still the only one who notices him.

"Now," he says. "Focus. Maybe you need to stop looking at Lizzy and pay attention to who else is looking at her, hmmm?" His grin widens and his black eyes sparkle. "Woolgather on your own time, Sweet Cheeks. Nighttime is my time!"

Dimly, I hear the conversation around me. I even hear myself speak to Bobby, but my eyes are doing as Sam commands. I'm watching the crowd, looking to see who's looking at my little girl.

At first, I notice nothing amiss. But as Bobby grabs me and whispers in my ear, I spot him. Will Harton, the man police say was responsible for Lizzy's abduction. He stalks out of the corn maze, heading past the prize booths and food vendors. Heading straight towards us in his burlap scarecrow mask, flannel shirt, and jeans. For an instant, he stares at Lizzy, who immediately steps behind her father and grabs his leg. Bobby swoops her up, making her squeal. He grabs her cheeks, forcing her to make duck lips.

"But look how cuuuuuuute!"

This time I don't look at her. I watch Harton. He strides past us, past the petting zoo and the restrooms. Then he disappears from my sight.

"Notice anything?"

Smilin' Sam is now dressed as a detective, with a trench-coat and a huge magnifying glass. He peers at me through it, making his black-button eye huge.

"He was staring at her," I say.

Sam yawns. "What else?"

When I don't say anything, he pulls a huge stopwatch from his pocket. It begins to tick.

"He was moving away from the corn maze!" I blurt, terri-fied of what will happen if I don't supply an answer.

"Aaaaaand?"

I look at him blankly for a moment, then it dawns on me.

"His trenchcoat! He wasn't wearing his trenchcoat!"

Ding Ding Ding, a bell rings in my ear, and Sam beams.

"Well, whattaya know! Even a broken clock is right twice a day!"

To my frustration, I wake up. The *Ding Ding Ding* is the bleat of my alarm clock, and the sunlight streaming through the window makes it impossible to go back to sleep. I have an appointment with my lawyer, Rick Eastman, this morning, anyway.

I still haven't told Bobby or the kids about my diagnosis. I know I'll have to, and soon, but I'm not ready. This family has endured so much heartbreak, and here I stand, ready to deliver the next blow. I'm determined to put it off as long as possible.

I was an only child, and my parents left me a more than adequate inheritance. The day after my diagnosis, I'd sat down with a hospital social worker and planned out the palliative care I would soon require. Creutzfeldt-Jakob Disease is rapidly progressive and always fatal. Dementia on speed, Dr. Hall had said. A neurodegenerative disorder that will burn through my brain, leaving nothing in its wake. In a matter of months, I will likely be comatose. I won't place the responsibility of my care on my children or my ex-husband.

At least the lack of hope simplifies how I'll spend my last days. I will make this as easy as I can for my family, from arranging my care in a facility of my choosing to making my funeral and burial plans. I'd discussed the latter with Rick years ago, but today when we meet, I'll ensure I have all the paperwork updated and in order. With that out of the way, I can focus on Elizabeth.

As I drive to Rick's office, I think about my dream and wonder if it means anything or if it is even real. Assuming it is, who is to say that Harton was the only scarecrow there that night? It had been Halloween, after all. Yet, somehow I know the masked scarecrow in my dream was him. Even though my thoughts are sometimes confusing these days, I remember the day I met him clearly.

Unbeknownst to Bobby, I'd visited Harton in jail after his arrest. I'd braced myself for a monster, and found a scared eighteen-year-old kid instead.

WILL Harton had immediately agreed with my request to meet him. They'd placed him in shackles on one side of a table in the interrogation room and I'd sat on the other. Officers watched us through the glass. I was sure they were recording everything, but I'd asked to speak with him alone.

"You know who I am?" I asked, and he nodded.

"Yes, Ma'am."

"Then you know what I want." My voice cracked and I felt a tear escape down my cheek. "Please ... just tell me where you left her. I know she's not alive. Just give her back to me, please."

He looked so young. How was a boy like this capable of what the sheriff assured me he'd done? He was handsome in a rough sort of way—tall, thin, with unkempt blond hair and eyes as blue as Elizabeth's. Those eyes bored into me, unwavering.

"Mrs. Bryant, I swear I didn't take her. I never touched your daughter."

"I'll talk to the D.A.," I begged, and forced myself to take the hand that had ended my daughter's life. "I'll ask them for a reduced sentence, a plea deal if you'll tell me where her body is. I'll get it in writing."

"Mrs. Bryant, no touching the prisoner, please," a voice boomed over the intercom.

When I tried to release his fingers, he grasped mine, maintaining contact.

"It wasn't me," he said. "I didn't do it. Someone took my coat when I went to break. I didn't take your daughter."

Cops swarmed into the room, forcing him to let go of my hand.

"This sack of shit isn't going to admit to anything," the sheriff said. "This meeting is over."

Harton shouted as they dragged him away, "Mrs. Bryant, please! I didn't do it. I'm innocent!"

The meeting left me shaken and unsure. I'd meant what I'd said about the plea agreement. I would beg the D.A. for a reduced sentence if he'd give us her body. Why would Harton risk the death penalty when I was giving him a way out?

The sheriff dismissed my doubts with a wave of his hand.

"Some people just can't accept what they've done. Everybody in this jail will tell you they're innocent. We see it all the time. But innocent men don't have a bag packed in their truck, ready to skip town. Innocent men don't lie about their alibi and have blood evidence on their clothing. Mrs. Bryant, I'd appreciate it if you don't share this with the press, but this man was arrested just weeks ago for a sexual offense against a minor and unlawful restraint. Unfortunately, the case got thrown out. But I'm telling you, this is our guy."

That had been enough for me at the time, but now, the

doubts are back. Am I catching everything Smilin' Sam is trying to show me?

I squeeze my eyes shut, wondering if this is part of my mental collapse. I'm pondering clues from a dream with a cartoon guide as if they are facts. Maybe this is how the end of my life will be, trapped in nightmare delusion until there is no reality left.

Still, Harton had felt wrong to me at the time. If he was a liar, he was the best I've ever seen. There was also his girlfriend. I remembered her from his preliminary hearing. Pretty, red-haired. She'd been dragged from the courtroom, screaming that they'd been together when Elizabeth disappeared and that no one, even Harton's lawyer, listened to her. The judge had threatened her with contempt and told her she'd have her chance to testify at the trial, but it had never come to that. Will Harton had been murdered in his cell a few weeks later, still awaiting his day in court.

I'd been unable to share these doubts with Bobby. That had hurt, since we'd once shared everything. Elizabeth's kidnapping had sent us hurtling in opposite directions. He'd stayed full of anger and alcohol and I'd retreated somewhere deep within myself. He had not taken out his aggression on us, however. He'd saved that for strangers in bar fights.

Let me be clear about that, to whomever might read this after I pass. Our divorce had nothing to do with falling out of love or any kind of wrongdoing. To this day, I love Bobby Bryant as much as I did the day we wed, and I know he still loves me. I divorced him because he needed more than I had left to give. Neither of us have made it back to the people we were before that night, and the only person to blame for that is our daughter's kidnapper.

The news of Harton's death gave Bobby a savage satisfaction that would've only been surpassed if he could've killed the boy himself. To me, it was another devastating loss, because if Will Harton had been the one who took Elizabeth, he had taken his knowledge of her whereabouts to his grave.

While I wait for my lawyer to collect me from his waiting area, I search Will Harton on my phone. It takes me a few articles, but I finally find one that lists his girlfriend, Alison Anderson.

The unincorporated town of Pelham, Tennessee has a population of less than 500 even today, so I think I might have a chance at finding her, even if Anderson is no longer her surname. To my surprise, I find her address right away on one of those people search sites, and after I finish my business with Rick, I decide to pay her a visit.

I pull up in front of a small, tidy white house and look around for dogs. Seeing none, I make my way up the porch steps. I have my hand raised to knock when the front door swings open.

Will Harton stands there, looking at me in surprise.

I THINK I SCREAM. I'm not sure. Clamping my eyes shut, I whisper, "You're not real."

When I open my eyes, he still stands there, staring. Half-expecting Smilin' Sam to appear and tell me to *'focus,* Catherine,' I choke back a sob and turn to flee. I almost fall down his steps in my attempt to retreat.

"Wait!" he says. "I know who you are. Mrs. Bryant, Will Harton was my father."

This stops me on the bottom step.

"Will Harton had a son?" Slowly, I turn to look at him. For the first time, I notice the forearm crutches he wears.

"He didn't at the ... when it happened. I was born four months after his death. Please, I'd love to talk to you. I've wanted to for years, but I didn't know how to approach you. Would you like to come inside?"

Seeing my hesitation, he adds, "Or we can talk on the porch."

This time it isn't Smilin' Sam's voice screaming a warning in my head, it's Bobby's, but I ignore it as I climb back up the steps.

"My name is Daniel," he says.

I glance at him, then look away. He looks so incredibly like his father.

"Please, have a seat."

I nod and sink into one of the faded patio chairs.

"Does your mother live here? I'd like to speak with her as well."

"My mom died four years ago," he replies as he eases himself into a wooden rocking chair. "Cancer."

I force myself to look at him. "I'm sorry for your loss. May I ask how you know who I am?"

"My mother spent the rest of her life trying to clear my

father's name. I've seen pictures of you, and television interviews. I saw the thirty-year anniversary special on Dateline."

Even ten years feels like a lifetime ago. With the rising popularity of true crime, Bobby and I have been approached by different shows over the years. I typically accept any opportunity to talk about her, praying for anything that might jog a memory or open up a new lead.

"You're versed in the case, then?" I ask, and he nods.

"There's a whole room in this house dedicated to Mom's research on the case. She did more work than the police ever did, I promise you."

"So, she still claimed she was with him when the abduction occurred?" I ask.

He looks at me. "Yes. That's why she fought so hard, even after he was gone. She wanted to clear his name."

"I talked to your father once," I admit. "I begged him to tell me where her body was. That was all I wanted. I told him I'd ask the D.A. for a plea bargain, but he didn't waiver for a moment. He said he didn't do it. I almost believed him. But the sheriff was absolutely positive it was him."

"I'll bet he was," Daniel says with a sigh. "You don't know, do you?"

"Know what?"

"Sheriff Anderson was my grandfather."

I BLINK AT HIM, unsure if I heard correctly. "I'm sorry?"

"My mother, Alison, was Sheriff Anderson's only daughter. He objected to their relationship to the point he'd tried to put my dad in jail for statutory rape and kidnapping in the summer of 1984, when they'd gotten caught at a motel in a neighboring town. My dad was from a rough family, not good enough for her, or so my grandfather thought. She was three weeks shy of her 17th birthday and he'd turned eighteen that spring."

"That's the sex offense he told me about?" I ask, dumbfounded.

Anderson was a common surname in our area, and it never once occurred to me that Will Harton's girlfriend and the sheriff might be related.

"He told you about that? He wasn't supposed to. Romeo and Juliet laws weren't in effect in 1984, but the D.A. had told him wasn't going to prosecute that. The sheriff had to let him go."

"What about his alibi?" I ask. "The sheriff said Harton lied about his alibi and had a bag packed, ready to flee town."

Daniel lifts his eyebrows. "Well, he did lie about his alibi at first, because he was with my mom. The sheriff had threatened my dad if he caught them together again, and even threatened to send Mom away if they didn't break off the relationship. They did, for a little while, but Mom found out she was pregnant and they rekindled things. They were planning on running away after he got paid that night. Old man McDowell always paid them in cash at closing and he paid a bonus if they worked Halloween. Mom told my grandmother she was at a party and would be home by midnight. They were hoping for a head start."

I frown. "So, why did she come that early? Lizzy disappeared around 7:40. That was more than two hours before closing."

Daniel gives me a long look, then he sighs. "I swore to myself, if I ever got the chance to talk to you, I'd tell you the truth, so I'm not going to sugarcoat this. I have my mother's version of that night's events inside, on video, if you want to hear her recount the story herself. I only ask that you don't think badly of her. She was just a kid, pregnant and terrified of her father. She did something dumb that night. She'd worked at the maze herself, the season before, in the ticket office. That's actually how my parents' relationship began. She knew how often they did the money drops, and how to access the safe. She was planning on stealing the night's receipts."

He pauses, as if waiting for my reaction, but I keep my face blank.

"She actually did, and sent someone into the maze to tell my father to meet her in the employee parking lot. He thought something was wrong, since she was there early, and he left his post to meet her. Without his coat and hat."

My mind flashes to Will Harton, glancing at Elizabeth as he stalked by us. Was that where he was going then, to meet Alison?

"My dad panicked when she showed him the money and made her put it back. He knew the sheriff was already gunning for him and didn't want to give him any legitimate charges to use against them. He also told Mom that wasn't how he wanted to start their life together. So, together, they managed to return the money. That's why there was never a report of the theft, and why both my father and mother initially lied about their whereabouts when your daughter was taken. They didn't know a child had been abducted. When the police questioned them, they thought somehow the police had found out about the money, even though it was returned. I also think it's why my father might've failed his lie detector test, though I've never had access to it."

Everything he says sounds plausible, but I want to see the video. I want to see her face as she tells the story. Daniel seems eager to oblige as he invites me inside.

Again, Bobby's voice screams a warning in my head as I enter the aging home ahead of Daniel. I'm so jumpy that I half-expect Daniel to throw down his forearm braces and attack me once we get inside, but he seems almost as nervous as I am.

The home is neat, if sparsely decorated. I glance at the pictures of a younger Daniel and his mother as we walk through the living room.

"This house was my maternal great-grandmother's," Daniel says. "She took Mom in after that night. Mom never lived in her father's house again and he was never a part of my life. When I was born with cerebral palsy, he told my mother it was because I was the son of a monster."

"I'm so sorry," I murmur.

Daniel shrugs. "It's okay. I think he really did believe my father was guilty, so I can't fault him for hating him—and by extension—me. In his eyes, we both ruined my mother's life. But I think his hatred of my father blinded him to things about that night that didn't fit his narrative. I think after he found the coat, he never even considered anyone else."

We walk down a hallway and he opens a closed bedroom door. Inside are two filing cabinets, a desk with chairs on either side, and an old TV/VCR combo on a cart. Daniel nods at one of the chairs and I take a seat.

"Everything in this room has to do with my father's case," he says. "Other than taking care of me, this became her life's work."

I glance at the filing cabinets, reading the labels on the drawers. Staff interviews, news coverage, evidence, possible suspects, and family interviews.

"She collected everything she could," Daniel says. "She went behind the police and interviewed all the people working that night. Only two of them refused to talk to her at all."

He reaches into the first cabinet and hands me a file from the front of the drawer. The first thing I look at is a stapled, two-page list. In the same neat handwriting, she has two columns. The left side lists a name and the right, their job title. She had also, somehow acquired copies of the timecards from that week, which had mechanical stamped IN and OUT times and had drawn out a map of the attraction with each booth meticulously labeled.

"She has a file on each of these people. What they remembered, what they saw, anything she could glean about their personal lives. You are welcome to look over all of it."

He taps on the possible suspects drawer. "Three of the people working that night had prior criminal convictions. One was for marijuana, one was a car theft and another was aggravated assault. That was Carter McCall, and my mother classified him as a possible suspect. He was working in a food booth that night. She also has files on people who lived in the area. One, Grady Morrison, was a convicted pedophile. He'd molested his own daughter, who was six at the time. As far as I know, the police never questioned him. He lived less than a mile from the maze. There was also a serial killer who was operating in Tennessee, Georgia, and Florida at the time, though his youngest known victim was 12 and the oldest 19. He was executed in Georgia in 2002."

He pulls open one of the drawers and runs his fingers over the spines of the stacked VCR tapes before selecting one. He turns on the TV/VCR combo and inserts the tape.

I'M no body language expert, but Alison Anderson seems earnest and open in her account of what had happened that night. When she talks about the attempted theft, she looks contrite and ashamed.

"I was wrong," she says. "I was just panicking. I knew Will and I would need all the money we could get until we got on our feet in Chattanooga, and I also knew that Mr. McDowell had so much it wouldn't hurt him. After I stole the money and put the bank bag in my purse, I ran into Kelly Jones as he came out of the restroom. I asked him to tell Will to meet me by his truck. When Will came to me, he was wearing his mask, but not his coat or hat. He asked me if I was okay and I showed him the money bag."

She sighs and her face reddens. "Will was horrified. He said he didn't want us to start our life together with stolen money and that we had to put it back. He also said my father would hang him if we were caught, which we most certainly would be. Will stood guard for me while I broke back into the barn office, where the safe was located. I put the money back and prayed that would be the end of it. Will said no matter what, don't admit to it if we were questioned. He told me he'd meet me after he got paid, as we originally planned. So, I drove back to my friend Ada Raulston's house and waited. Will never came, but the police did. When they asked me where I'd been that evening, I panicked and lied. I said that I'd been at Ada's since 6:00 p.m., and she backed me up. Her mom was at work, so it was just us there. By the time we found out they were investigating an abduction, not a robbery, I went to the station and tried to tell the truth. Ada did, too. But they weren't listening to us anymore. Will had lied to them at first, too, but when he realized how serious it was, he'd told them he'd been with me. They didn't believe him, either, and my father was furious. Everything happened so fast ..."

The tape ends and Daniel looks at me. "I mean, I wasn't there and I don't know, but I don't understand why she would lie about it all these years. Not to protect me, because I was still known as the murderer's crippled son. I was bullied so much we even left here for a while, but we came back when great-grandma got sick. I was a senior in high school. Mom took care of her the last two years of her life, and great-grandma left her this place. Like I said, you're free to look through all these files—and I hope you do. I can't understand why she would do this much work if her story wasn't true."

"Maybe she was in love with him and didn't want it to be?" I say.

Daniel concedes the point and says, "You and I, we're in the same boat in a way. If my father was innocent, he lost his life because of that night. I won't compare his death to the loss of your child. I can't even imagine what you've been through. But that night affected everything about my life and my mother's as well. I'm at the point—whether he's guilty or innocent—I just want to know the truth. I feel like you want that, too, or you wouldn't be here."

"You're right," I admit. "I'm dying, Daniel. I just want to find her. That is my last wish in this world."

His face creases. "I'm so sorry. Cancer?"

I didn't plan on telling him about it. I hate the sympathy on his face. I'd received a lifetime of sympathy and it had never helped anything. That is another reason I'm putting off telling Bobby and the boys. I'm so sick of being pitied and helpless. But there is something about Daniel ... he is right. We share an awful, tragic kinship. Maybe we can work together and find the answers we both need.

I tell him briefly about Creutzfeldt-Jakob Disease and about the dream, omitting the part about Smilin' Sam because that feels crazy to admit, even as a dream creation. It is still enough to make me seem insane, I suppose, but Daniel merely looks thoughtful.

"Well, I read about a case once where a witness was hypnotized to remember a license plate number. I think our brains hold onto more information than we know how to recall sometimes. I've never had access to any of the police files. I thought I would be able to get them, especially since they consider the case closed, but—"

"What do you mean, closed?" I interrupt.

"I went to the jail after my grandfather died and a new sheriff was appointed. Bradley, I think. He told me the case was closed. They were sure they had their guy and he was deceased, but he refused to give me access to any of the reports or my father's polygraph results."

The words leave me stricken. Although I know Lizzy's case is cold, I thought she was a file on someone's desk, that there is still a chance some officer someday would reopen it and maybe find something we'd all missed before. The thought of her filed away, dismissed yet never found, dismays me, then makes me furious.

"Maybe they'll give the files to me," I say. "Want to go for a ride?"

"HERE GOES NOTHING," Daniel says, as we walk into the station. A bored looking officer at the desk mutters, "Can I help you?" around a mouthful of fries.

"We'd like to see the sheriff, please," I say.

"And you are?"

"Catherine Bryant and ..." I pause, unsure of which surname Daniel goes by.

"Daniel Harton," he supplies.

SMILIN' SAM'S CORN MAZE

"What's it concerning?" the officer asks, then slurps his shake loudly.

"An old murder investigation," I reply.

That, at least, seems to draw his attention away from his meal.

"Just a sec and I'll see if she's busy," he says and lifts a receiver.

Daniel and I look at each other. A new sheriff, maybe a new opportunity? In the beginning, I'd worked so hard to keep Lizzy's case active. I'd called the police every week, talked to every media person who would talk to me ... but week after week of no new information had eventually defeated me. I feel ashamed that there are at least two county sheriffs I've never spoken to about Lizzy.

A pretty woman with dark hair and eyes follows the officer back to his desk. She offers a smile and a handshake.

"I'm Sheriff Lucia Alvarez," she says.

"Catherine Bryant and Daniel Harton," I answer. "We'd like to talk to you about Elizabeth Bryant. She was abducted on Halloween in—"

"The kid from the corn maze!" the male officer blurts, and Alvarez frowns at the over-enthusiastic tone of his voice.

"It's the most famous case around here," he says sheepishly. "I grew up terrified of cornfields because of it."

Sheriff Alvarez, who looks as though she probably hadn't been born when Lizzy was taken, says, "Why don't we go back to my office?"

Once we are seated, she says, "How can I help you?"

"Elizabeth was my daughter. She was never found.

Daniel's father was the man arrested for kidnapping her and he was killed in custody."

Sheriff Alvarez blinks, but merely says, "Go on."

"We've been discussing the case and think there might have been some things missed in the initial investigation. According to Daniel, the case was closed upon his father's death. If that's true, I'd like to request copies of the file. Also, that the evidence be released to me."

The sheriff taps something on her laptop and frowns.

"Excuse me for just a moment," she says and leaves the office.

She's gone for nearly twenty minutes. When she returns, she looks annoyed.

"Unfortunately, it looks like the evidence was destroyed."

Daniel makes a muffled sound of distress and she exhales.

"I know. I'm upset, too. Your father was never convicted, and Elizabeth was never recovered. Protocol states that the evidence should've been kept and the case should remain open. DNA was never run on the coat or underwear, of course, because the technology didn't exist then. But it would be nice to have it to test now. We only know the blood types found on the clothing."

"There was more than one?" Daniel asks.

"Yes," the sheriff says. "Do you happen to know your father's blood type?"

"No," he admits.

"Elizabeth's was A positive," I say. " I know because I have the Rh factor and three of my kids had to have the Rhogam shot."

The sheriff jots it on a notepad and says, "I admit, I've never reviewed this case because it was logged in the computer as closed. I'm not sure why that happened."

"I bet I can guess," Daniel says.

"What do you mean?"

"Tell her," I urge him. "Tell her everything you've told me today."

Sheriff Alvarez looks floored when he finishes. She stares at Daniel for a long moment, then scribbles something on her notepad. Ripping off the page, she stands and says, "Excuse me again."

Then she stalks out of the room.

Daniel and I look at each other.

"Don't get your hopes up," I warn. "This office has never offered much of that."

But when Sheriff Alvarez comes back, she carries a box. The same desk officer from before follows on her heels, carrying two bottles of cold water, which he offers us. He looks like he wants to linger, but one glare from Alvarez sends him scurrying. He pulls the door shut behind him.

She sets the box on her desk and extracts three files.

"This is what we have left—" she begins.

The sight of those three thin files makes me flash hot with anger.

"I thought you said just the evidence was destroyed. Where's the rest of it?"

Sheriff Alvarez looks angry, too. But when she speaks, I realize it isn't directed at me.

"I know, Mrs. Bryant. That's what I thought, too. It

seems inconceivable to me that this is all that was documented in an abducted child investigation, so maybe there's another box stored in the basement. I promise you, I'll go look for myself. But this box is all that's logged in the system."

"His mother has *two filing cabinets* full, and—"

Daniel lays a hand on my wrist. "What's in the files, Sheriff?"

She flips open the first one. "This is your father's intake form, fingerprints ... catalog of personal effects he had on him at the time of arrest." She shoots him an apologetic look. "His autopsy report. Photos."

Daniel reaches for the file, but she hesitates. "You don't want to see this."

"I never met him," Daniel says tersely. "It's fine."

She hands the file to him and I peer over his shoulder. I wince at the photo of Will Harton lying lifeless on a morgue table. The words BABY KILLER are carved into his pale chest and ugly red ligature marks bite into his throat.

"I thought he was stabbed," Daniel murmurs, flipping to the autopsy report. Then he nods and says, "Yep. That was the cause of death. Apparently, the lynching failed."

He tries to keep his face impassive, but I see him flinch as he flips through the photos. They look so much alike. Whether Daniel knew him or not, this has to be difficult. For an instant, I picture Lizzy lying there, small and battered, dark, sweaty bangs plastered against her eerily pale forehead.

"Did they even bother to try to find out who did this?" Daniel asks. "My mother never knew."

Alvarez gives a terse head shake. "The incident report cites 'multiple assailants' but no one was ever charged."

The next file contains a transcript of Will Harton's polygraph and the analyst's conclusions. We watch as Sheriff Alvarez scans them while trying to explain to us how polygraph testing works, with its relevant questions, control questions, irrelevant questions, and concealed information questions. Then she trails off in the middle of her sentence and softly says, "Shit."

She flips through the pages, then back again. Then she hands the file across her desk. I let Daniel take it and scoot my chair close to his to read over his shoulder.

"As you suspected, he failed the questions about his whereabouts and alibi miserably. But on every single question about Elizabeth, he passed," the Sheriff says.

Daniel and I look up at her, then at each other. We both read over the questions anyway, needing to see for ourselves.

"I'll be contacting the FBI and TBI, to see if they conducted their own investigations and have anything else we can access, but there's no notation in the computer of that. I'm reopening this investigation." Her dark eyes flash with intensity. "I know it's a lot to ask, considering how this case has been handled so far, but I'd like a chance to investigate. I know this county and these people. I think I have a better chance at getting them to talk than the feds, but if you want to bring them in first, I completely understand."

I study her, sensing her drive, her fire. I want that on our side. I glance at Daniel and he gives me a slight nod.

"We want you to investigate first," I say.

She exhales. "Give me a couple of weeks. If I can't find anything by then, I'll call in the FBI myself."

The final file contains witness statements. At first, we find nothing remarkable. One of the maze workers, Jason Thompkins, reported that Will had acted nervous that night, quiet and hyper-alert. He also reported that Will wasn't at his assigned post around the time Lizzy went missing, but there is no mention of the trench coat or hat. Most other people simply state that they saw nothing, though the worker at the shooting match game verified Bobby's statement about Corey's nosebleed and how Corey, Lizzy, and I had gone to the restrooms together. He reported that was the last time he saw Lizzy. A man named Alan Barnes verified he'd seen Corey hurrying towards the restrooms, with me and Lizzy chasing behind him.

I close my eyes for a second, trying not to think about what happened next. It seems so cruel, so inconceivable, that so much could be lost in a matter of minutes. All because of one stupid mistake.

My mistake.

I open my eyes.

Stop it, Cathi, I tell myself. *You cannot dwell on this. Not now.*

I've spent decades dwelling on it.

That's right, Smilin' Sam's voice whispers. *Focus.*

Determined, I scan the next witness statement, then the next. The one on the last page stops me cold.

A man named Larry Brown, who was there with his son, stated he saw a little dark-haired girl with pigtails talking to a scarecrow with a straw hat and trench coat at the edge of the maze. The scarecrow offered his hand and she took it, following him into the maze.

"That's not what Sheriff Anderson told us," I say. "He said the scarecrow picked her up and ran into the maze." I pause, turning it over in my mind, then I shake my head. "Lizzy wouldn't have done that. She would've been scared of him."

"I want to talk to this witness," Sheriff Alvarez says. "This statement directly implicated Will Harton. If you're correct—"

"If Lizzy didn't take his hand and walk into the corn maze, Larry Brown was lying," Daniel states. "Sheriff, do you know this person? Do you think this person even exists?"

I give him a sharp look. "Surely you don't think Sheriff Anderson went that far to implicate your father, fabricating witnesses?"

Daniel merely shrugs.

"I don't know that name," Sheriff Alvarez says. "But I'll get to work on it. If he is a real person, I'll need to check his criminal record, interview him to exclude him as a suspect as well."

I blink at her. Maybe Bobby was right in his jubilation at the thought of Elizabeth's killer's death. The thought of this person running free for nearly forty years—doing God knows what to God knows who—makes me suddenly, violently ill. Daniel must notice because he asks, "Mrs. Bryant, are you okay?"

I nod. For Lizzy, I have to be strong.

Daniel grabs one of the files again. "My father's blood type isn't listed in the autopsy report?"

"Unfortunately, no. And there's likely nothing else on file at the M.E. office after this long. If we had any evidence to compare it to, we could use your DNA to possibly exclude him, but ..." She shakes her head. "Are your paternal grandparents alive?"

Daniel frowns. "My grandfather, but we're not really close."

"Well, if he could tell you where your father was born, or remember the doctor's name, the blood type might be in some old file, but that in itself won't be enough to prove guilt or innocence. Can I get both of your addresses and phone numbers?"

She pushes a pad of paper and a pen across to us, and we scribble our information.

"Daniel, I'd like to stop by soon and see your mother's files, if that's okay?" the sheriff asks. "I'll give you advance notice. But I think I need to track down this eyewitness first."

"Yes, anytime," he says quickly.

The sheriff stands and offers a sympathetic smile. "Okay, I promise to keep you both updated. Now, maybe you should go get some rest, Mrs. Bryant. You look tired."

I *am* tired. Exhausted. And—as much as Smilin' Sam scares me—I look forward to the nightmare tonight, to see if he can give me any further information. I stand and offer her my hand.

"Thank you, Sheriff."

Daniel also shakes her hand and thanks her for her time. I

like the fire I see in her dark eyes. I feel like she will really try, and that gives me more hope than I've had in decades.

"I'll be in touch," she says. "Soon."

IN THE PARKING LOT, a violent orange sun is sinking. What a day this has been.

We are quiet for the first part of the drive to Daniel's house, then he murmurs, almost to himself, "My God, Mrs. Bryant, I really don't think he did it."

"I really don't, either," I admit.

The same thought that gives him such relief causes another surge of nausea in my stomach. I try to look at the bright side. If this man is out there, still alive, then there is a chance he could tell us where Lizzy is. That's all I want ... right?

As I pull in front of Daniel's house, the streetlights are coming on. He shoots me a concerned look. "Are you okay to drive? I could drive you home in my van and you could come back to collect your car tomorrow."

"I'll be fine," I assure him. "I don't live far from here."

He grabs a pen from my console and writes his number on a fast food napkin. "Well, call me when you get home, so I know you're okay, please."

I nod and he climbs out of the car, adjusting his braces. "And Mrs. Bryant ... thank you for this. I'll do everything I can to help you find her."

This whole thing feels like a dream. My thoughts are hazy,

troubled. The more I go over it in my head, the less I believe Will Harton was guilty. How will Bobby react?

A car flashes its high beams at me and I realize I bright-lighted them first. I flip on my low beams and turn both the radio and the air conditioner on.

The oldies station is playing *Drive* by The Cars.

Ric Ocasek's crooning voice fills me with trepidation and I punch the power button again, killing the sound. I am child-ishly afraid to glance over to the passenger seat.

A truck blares its horn at me as I cross the yellow line and I jerk the wheel back to the right, almost over-correcting.

"Arrive alive! Don't let Cathi drive!" Smilin' Sam cries from the backseat. His grinning face fills my rearview mirror.

"What are you doing here?" I screech, somehow keeping my car out of the ditch.

"Awww, Kit-Kat. You act like you aren't happy to see me," he clucks. "I told you, I'm here to help you get your shit together. It's looking like that might be a 24/7 proposition."

His words fill me with terror. I can't handle this ... *abomi-nation* ... during my waking hours, too.

I'm almost home. Thank God. I nearly miss the driveway, stomping on my brakes to make the sharp turn.

"Hells Bells!" Sam shouts as the sudden movement makes him tumble around the backseat.

I sit in the driveway, staring at my house, my heart thud-ding in my chest.

Then I see her. Lizzy, running around the side of the house, chasing lightning bugs. She runs up to my car, stop-ping mere feet from me. A burly man steps out of the shadows of the house, coming from the same direction. I don't recognize his face.

"Hey!" he yells. "Come back here!"

Lizzy glances at him, her smile fading, then back at me. She stares at me curiously, with no sign of recognition.

He starts walking faster, closing the gap between them.

I THROW OPEN THE DOOR. "LIZZY!" I hiss. "Get in!"

To my horror, she shakes her head and backs toward the man, who is now sprinting toward her.

"Lizzy, please!" I cry. "He's coming!"

"Daddy!" she shouts, and turns to reach for him, her blond braid swinging.

Blond.

I blink at the two strangers, confused.

The man grabs the little girl up and she slings her arms around his neck. It isn't Lizzy. I don't know either of them. But the house ... this is *my* house.

"What the hell are you trying to do, lady?" the man yells.

"What are you doing at my house?" I demand. "Who are you?"

"Hank?"

A thin blonde woman steps onto the porch. "Is everything alright?"

"No!" he says. "Call the police."

"This is *our* house," the man says, but he frowns as he approaches, studying my face. "Lady ... are you okay?"

I stare back at the house. It is green now, not blue. I don't recognize the swingset in the yard, or the pink flowers bordering the porch.

It had been my house, once. But not for decades. I glance in the backseat. No Sam. Then I burst into tears.

"I'm sorry!" I cry. "I got confused. I used ... I used to live here, with my husband and sons and my ... my little girl. I thought ..."

"Hey! It's okay," he says, his face softening.

"Go to Mama," he whispers to the little girl and sets her down. She scampers toward the lady on the porch, who is talking on the phone.

"Do you have someone I can call for you?" he asks kindly.

I don't know where my phone is, but the napkin is there with Daniel's name and number. I thrust it at him and he pulls a phone from his back pocket.

He turns away so I can't hear the conversation. I lay my head on the steering wheel and cry.

I don't know how long I sit there before I hear the sirens and the police car pulls in behind me. I glance up to see Sheriff Alvarez talking to the man. He gestures at the little girl watching from the porch, then at me. She says something to him and walks over to me.

"Mrs. Bryant," she says gently. "Are you okay?"

"I ... I got confused," I say. "I'm so sorry."

"Do you have someone I could call?" she asks.

"I've already called someone for her," the man says. "Daniel? He said he was on his way."

"I'm here," I hear Daniel say breathlessly, as he makes his way up the driveway with his crutches. "Is she okay?"

"Mrs. Bryant got confused," the sheriff says. "She thought this was her house, and that little girl was Elizabeth."

"Well, she told him that this *was* her house, once," Daniel says. "Mrs. Bryant has Creutzfeldt-Jakob Syndrome. It's an aggressive type of dementia."

"I see," the sheriff says sympathetically. "Mrs. Bryant, do you want us to call anyone else? Your husband?"

"We're divorced," I say.

"I'll take her home," Daniel says, then glances at me. "That is, if you can give me the address."

I rattle it off to him.

"I can get one of my officers to drive her car and follow you guys," the sheriff says, then turns back to me. "Mr. Lane here says he doesn't want to press charges, but you can't be showing up here trying to put his daughter in a car, okay?"

"Okay," I murmur, my mouth dry.

Dear God, I had tried to take that little girl, just like someone had taken mine.

"I think it would be a good idea if you don't drive anywhere by yourself anymore, either. Will you promise me that?"

"I—I promise," I say.

Soon, we are on our way, our own little parade through town. Daniel and I lead in his van, an officer behind him driving my car and the sheriff bringing up the rear.

"I'm so sorry," I tell Daniel.

He reaches over and squeezes my hand. "Don't be sorry. I'm sorry this is happening to you."

We all enter my apartment. I feel humiliated, wondering what my neighbors must think.

The sheriff, Daniel, and I sit in the living room.

"What happened tonight could've been very serious," Sheriff Alvarez says. "You could've been hurt, or hurt someone."

"I know," I say. "It's the first time it's happened. It's a recent diagnosis."

"You're probably going to need to appoint a conservator," she says. "Do you have a family member that I can contact?"

"I haven't told them yet," I admit. "I spent the first part of today getting my affairs in order. I didn't realize it would happen this fast. I'll tell them tomorrow."

"Is it alright if I take your keys?" the sheriff asks. "Any of them can pick them up at the station. I just don't want you getting confused and getting in your car and getting hurt."

"Can you give them to Daniel?" I ask, and she shakes her head.

"I'd rather give them to a family member, Mrs. Bryant. Is that okay with you?"

I sigh. "Yes."

"I'm going to hang out a little while," Daniel says. "Make sure she's good before I take off."

"Okay," the sheriff says. "You two take care."

When she leaves, Daniel says, "Hey, are you really okay? Can I get you anything?"

I give him a thin smile. "I'm starving."

38

He grins. "Oh, God, me too! How about I order us a pizza?"

"That sounds wonderful," I replied, and he asks what kind I like before he opens an app on his phone. He refuses to take any money for it.

"I dread telling them," I say as we wait. "This will kill Bobby."

"I thought you were divorced?" he asks.

"We divorced six years after Elizabeth was taken, but I never stopped loving that man. He never stopped loving me either. We raised our boys together and are still part of each other's lives. We just cope in different ways, I guess. I withdrew into myself and Bobby always hated being alone. I can't fault him for that."

Our pizza arrives and I tell him a story about Bobby's latest girlfriend, Ashley, as we eat. Bobby has had a dizzying array of girlfriends over the years, none of them serious. Some of them have tried to challenge our continuing friendship but none have been successful. Bobby tells them I am his children's mother and his best friend and if they can't accept that, they can move along. His last three girlfriends share a similar look and similar names: Ashley, Amanda, and Amelia.

Corey had thrown a surprise birthday party for Bobby's 70th and the newly minted girlfriend Ashley had been upset that I was invited. Bobby had gently explained that I was family, too, but she had only gotten louder and more tearful, until he said, "Amelia! I told you—" Then, realizing his mistake, he muttered, "Jesus Christ, here we go," under his breath just before she lit into him for calling her the wrong name. The twins started laughing first, then Josh, then Bobby. I tried to hold back my grin, but maybe not successfully enough, because she hissed, "At least he didn't call me *Catherine.*"

Josh rolled his eyes at her. "That's because he'd never get our mother confused with any of you."

She stormed off to the restroom.

"Should I go check on her?" I asked.

Bobby waved me off and handed me a piece of cake. "She'll be fine. She's just young and jealous."

"Dad, she's 62," Josh muttered, and we all cracked up then.

Now, anytime Ashley annoys them, the boys purposely call her the wrong name: Amy, Allie, Angie ... It never fails to enrage her.

"Oh, man!" Daniel chortles. "That's great." His smile fades and he says, "I'm glad you've still had some good times, too, and that you're still close. It's crazy how that one night changed so many lives."

We talk about what we've learned today, and he tells me, "As soon as I got home, I looked in the filing cabinet to see if Mom had interviewed Larry Brown. She hadn't."

We discuss our next moves and I get up to retrieve a notepad and pen from the kitchen. It only takes me a moment, but when I return, Daniel has his head laid back, asleep.

To my horror, Smilin' Sam crouches behind the couch, clutching my largest kitchen knife.

"WHAT IF YOU'RE WRONG?" Sam says. "What if Harton *was* the killer? Maybe we should kill this guy now, what do you think? Eye for an eye, tooth for a tooth?"

"Leave him alone!" I hiss.

Grinning, he draws the blade lightly across Daniel's throat. Blood beads in the shallow cut. Sam licks the blade with an obscenely bright pink tongue and proclaims, "Delicious!"

I WAKE WITH A START, my heart slamming in my chest. The lamp is off, but I can see Daniel, still in the same position.

Is he sleeping, or is he dead?

My hand brushes something cold in my lap and I realize it is the knife.

Daniel grunts in his sleep and stirs. Panicking, I shove the knife under the cushion I'm sitting on and snap on the light.

He winces and gives me a sheepish smile as he lifts his head.

"Sorry about that. I guess I crashed on you."

I try to speak, but my mouth is too dry. Relief crashes over me until he turns to look at the clock and I see the thin scratch across his neck.

"You look tired," he says. "Go get some rest and call me tomorrow."

Numbly, I walk him to the door and manage a goodbye. Then I bolt it behind him.

What is happening to me?

I'm afraid to go to sleep, but I'm so damn exhausted. I can't call anyone to come stay with me, because what if I (or Sam) were to murder them in their sleep?

But I need to see the rest of the dream. I change into my gown and go to bed, locking my bedroom door as well.

I'M BACK in the car, listening to Bobby singing *Drive*, but this time, Smilin' Sam sits on the middle seat beside Josh, drinking a cartoon carton of milk with Lizzy's face on the side. He gives me that ferocious grin when he catches me looking.

"You should've seen your face!" he says. "What a hoot!"

"I hate you," I whisper and he tries to look dismayed.

"Aw, c'mon Cath. It gets boring rolling around up here in your empty head. I gotta get my kicks somehow."

He snaps his fingers and suddenly I am sitting on a cartoon couch across from Sam, who is in a suit. A light turns on, blinding me, as Sam says in a serious announcer voice, "On today's episode of The Most Negligent Mothers of All-Time, we have Catherine, who lost her daughter in a corn maze 39 years ago ... AND HASN'T FOUND HER YET! What do you have to say for yourself, Catherine?"

An audience I can't see boos and hisses.

"Stop it!" I cry and Sam rolls his eyes.

He snaps his fingers again and we are standing just inside the gates of the corn maze. I watch Will Harton stalk past, staring at Elizabeth. She backs behind her father, grabbing his leg and Bobby bends down to swoop her up. She squeals and he grabs her cheeks, forcing her to do duck lips.

"But look how cuuuuuuuute!"

Dimly, I hear Josh and Bobby talk, see the twins laughing at the green slime hanging from their noses. Then Bobby takes my hand and smiles.

"You ready?" he asks.

We walk into the petting zoo first. The twins protest, but even they stop to pet the baby goats.

Suddenly, a Raggedy Andy steps forward and yells, "Hi, there!"

His high-pitched, squeaky voice is too much like Sam's, and so are his shiny dark eyes. I want to turn away, but I don't. He tells Lizzy to hold out her arm and when she does, he strikes her wrist with a slap bracelet. She squeals in delight as she admires the tiny black cats on the orange bracelet that now encircles her wrist.

"What do you tell him?" Bobby asks, and she shouts, "Thank you!"

"You're welcome!" he cries. "Hey! I like your shoes."

He points at Lizzy's mismatched sneakers and she giggles.

"Let's go to the maze!" Lizzy says.

"We told you," Caleb says. "It's not for babies."

"And I told *you*," Bobby says, "That Lizzy and I are going to beat you. But let's do that last, the big finale. How about some games?"

"Yes!!" all four kids cry in unison.

They throw darts first. Bobby wins an ugly, misshapen toy that was supposed to be E.T., I guess, and hands it to Lizzy. She hugs it to her like it is her prized possession.

"I love you more than watermelon," Bobby tells her and kisses her nose.

"I love you more than ..." She pauses to think, then her eyes grow wide. "ICE CREAM!"

Bobby matches her wide eyes. "That is a LOT!"

She beams at him and nods furiously.

Next, Bobby pays for them all to shoot mounted guns at pop-up targets. Lizzy doesn't participate, talking instead to her E.T. like it's a baby.

"Mom!" Josh cries, and points at Corey.

Blood flows from his nose, splattering the front of his Ghostbuster outfit. The twins have allergies and sometimes have random nosebleeds. The doctor had simply said, "Hormones, nothing to worry about."

"Oh, come on," I say, grabbing his hand. "Hold your head back."

He tilts his head back and lets me tug him toward the restrooms. Lizzy leaves E.T. beside Bobby and trails after us.

This is it. The moment of my worst mistake. I don't need Sam to tell me to focus. I am on hyper-alert, even though I can't do anything except observe.

A line winds outside the ladies room. I'm about to excuse myself to the front of it, just to get to the sink, when Corey says, "I am not going in there," and veers toward the men's room.

I chase after him and Lizzy chases after me.

"Go back to your father!" I hear myself tell her. Then I yell, "Bobby! She's with you!"

That night, I hadn't looked back to make sure he'd heard me. I was too concentrated on my bleeding son. Tonight, I do. Bobby, Caleb, and Josh are bent over their guns, waiting on the targets to pop up. I turn my head to watch Lizzy start back toward him. I want to scream at her, or at least pull her back to me, but I have no control.

I can only watch as her head whips toward the corn maze. I see a shadowy figure wave at her and yell something, though I can't hear what he says over the music. Lizzy hears him, though. She smiles, and with one more glance toward Bobby, she walks toward the maze.

I WAKE myself screaming her name. Immediately, I grab a notepad and jot down everything I can remember about the dream. Then I hurry to the living room, grab my phone and the paper on the coffee table, and call Daniel.

"Hey!" he says. "How are you feeling? I wanted to check on you after Sunday service, but I didn't want to bother you."

I frown, distracted by his statement. I glance out the window at the gray October sky and ask, "What time is it?"

"Nearly one. Are you okay?"

One o'clock. I can't remember ever sleeping that late in my life. It scares me, but I push that away.

"Do you remember if your mother questioned a Raggedy Andy? I think he spoke to Lizzy that night."

Daniel must sense my urgency, because he just says, "Hang on."

I hear the squeak of the filing cabinet drawer, then a rustle of papers. Finally he says, "No, I don't have anything on a Raggedy Andy. No time card, no interview. Do you know what part he worked in?"

"The petting zoo."

"Let me dig around some more and I'll call you back."

After we disconnect, I stare at the phone. I don't want to make this call, but I have to. I need someone else to confirm if Raggedy Andy existed, if any of these details existed, or if this is all in my head. Hesitantly, I call Bobby. He answers on the second ring.

"Hey, pretty girl," he says. He always calls me that, or darlin', no matter who is present.

"What are you doing?" I ask.

"Sittin' here watching the grass grow. What about you? It's good to hear your voice."

"I'm about to call the boys. I wonder if you can all meet me at my apartment? I need to talk to you about the night Lizzy disappeared."

There is silence on the other end of the line. I wait him out. Finally, he says, "Cath, why? What could we possibly say that we haven't said in the past forty years?"

"Please? It's urgent, and I'll explain when you get here."

"Will Harton is dead. Lizzy is ..." He clears his throat. "... never coming home. The police searched everywhere connected to him. Unless someone finds her by pure, blind luck, it's probably not going to happen. I don't understand why we have to keep torturing ourselves, and our kids—"

"Because I'm dying, Bobby," I blurt. "And when you lay my bones to rest, I want to be lying next to her."

"You're what?" he gasps, and I feel guilty for telling him like this, over the phone. Bobby will probably mourn me more than anyone. I had done the best I could, but I'd never again been the mother or wife I was before that night. Not the one they'd deserved.

Briefly, I tell him about Creutzfeldt-Jakob Disease and assure him that I am doing everything the doctor says. I ask if he can be here with me when I tell the boys and he says yes.

Our sons aren't as hard to convince to come over, especially when I tell them their father will be here as well.

Bobby arrives less than twenty minutes later. When I unlock the door, I catch a glimpse of his red-rimmed eyes just before he seizes me in his arms. I didn't realize how much I need that right now. How much I need him. I cling to him, feeling his wiry body tremble.

"Please don't," I whisper. "Please don't cry. I'm at peace with it. I just want to find our baby."

He doesn't say anything. I know he is wondering how we were supposed to do that after all this time, after zero leads, but I have hope. Maybe I can jog their memories. Maybe they can confirm mine.

"It's not supposed to be like this," he says, his voice muffled in my hair. "I told you, I wanted to go first."

"I'll save you a seat," I say, and he makes a sound that is a half-chuckle, half-sob. It is an inside joke and an old one.

I'D MOVED to town when I was fifteen and had immediately attracted the unwanted attention of a creepy neighborhood boy. When I spotted him boarding the school bus, I'd surreptitiously shifted my bookbag from my lap to the seat beside me.

"Well, hey, hot stuff," he said, then noticed my bag and frowned.

I frantically searched the faces of the other boarding passengers before locking eyes with a tall, skinny guy behind him. Pasting on a bright smile, I said, "Hey, I saved you a seat!"

The boy shot a confused look over his shoulder, then back at me before it dawned on him. He gave me a dazzling smile and said, "Thanks!"

The creep grunted and moved on and the boy plopped down beside me.

That was the moment I met Bobby Bryant. We've been saving seats for each other ever since.

Josh and Corey arrive at my apartment together, then Caleb. The smiles they always give when they see their father and I together fade when they notice his red eyes.

"Dad ..." Josh says tentatively. "Are you okay? Everything alright with your heart?"

Bobby had a heart attack last June, terrifying us all.

He shakes his head and turns away. Seeing him tear up makes a lump rise in my throat. I reach behind me and grasp his hand. His cold fingers squeeze mine.

"This time it's me," I say. "I've been diagnosed with Creutzfeldt-Jakob Disease."

I tell them what I know about it: progression, prognosis, my plans for palliative care when things get worse. I try to keep my voice calm, soothing, so maybe they won't be as upset. It doesn't work.

"Dammit, Mom, would you quit talking about this like it's the transmission slipping in your car?" Josh demands. "You're *dying*."

"I hate that voice," Caleb mutters, swiping at his eyes. "It's the same one you used when you told us you and Dad were getting divorced. For once, can you just *feel* something?"

"Boys—" Bobby says, his voice low and warning.

"It's true, Dad," Corey interjects. Looking at his twin, he says, "Can't you see? She *wants* to die. She checked out on us years ago. Might as well have buried her the night Lizzy—"

Josh shoves him, hard, knocking him against the wall. A picture of us—the last family picture we'd had made—falls. It shatters on the floor, as if to underscore how irreparably broken we are.

"Stop it!" Bobby shouts. "This is your mother. She's trying to be strong for you. For me. Like she always has. None of you will speak to her like that again as long as I'm alive."

The room falls silent and Caleb begins to cry. He hurls himself into my arms like a child and I hold him tight.

"I'm sorry, Mama," he sobs.

"It's okay. I love you," I whisper. "Everything's going to be okay."

When he lets go, I move to the couch and pat the seat beside me. Josh and Caleb flank me. Corey sits in the recliner and Bobby paces.

"The doctor said I might be a candidate for a new trial drug," I say. "I will do whatever he tells me to do."

Josh forces a smile and says, "If anyone's a fighter, it's you."

He glances at Corey, as if daring him to challenge that, but Corey just stares at his shoes. The twins had chosen to live with their father after the divorce and I didn't blame them. Only my firstborn had stayed with me, and I think it was mostly because he was afraid to leave me alone. Maybe Corey is right. Maybe I *had* checked out. On them, on my marriage … I'd never meant to. Lizzy's disappearance had gutted me. I hadn't known how to support them when I was drowning.

Aware that it might precipitate another argument, I continue, "So, I'm on this new treatment, and one of the side effects is these really vivid dreams—"

"You'll move in with me and Steph," Josh interrupts. "I'm not letting you go to a facility."

"Honey, I'm not going to be a burden on any of you. I have it all planned out, but that's not what I want to talk about. As I said, one of the side effects of the meds is vivid dreams. You wouldn't believe how vivid they are. I can smell things, feel them … " Swallowing hard, I say, "I've been dreaming about the night Lizzy was taken. I've remembered something that might be important, and I want to see if any of you remember it, too."

Corey purses his lips but doesn't say anything.

I plow ahead. "My dream starts in the same place every time. I'm going to describe it to you."

Reading from my notes, I walk them through our entry to the park, omitting the part about Smilin' Sam.

"You remember all of that?" Bobby asks. "What we were wearing, what we were eating ... even the songs playing in the background?"

"I didn't until I started having this dream. I have the same dream every night."

Bobby shoots me a horrified look.

"Some of it's not bad," I quickly reassure him. "I love seeing all of you when you were young. Corey, you were obsessed with Prince and were trying to grow the top of your hair out. You walked around with your collar flipped up."

Josh grins. "I remember that. You looked stupid."

Corey snorts, but he smiles, too.

"Your dad's hair was long and he was the most handsome man I'd ever seen. Even though he sang the wrong words to every song he ever listened to."

"Still does," Corey says, and Bobby scowls with pretended offense.

"My favorite is the Bon Jovi song," Caleb says. "It doesn't make a difference if we're naked or not. He sang in the car with me and Paula before Em was born and she laughed so hard I was afraid her water would break."

"Did you forget Karma Chameleon?" Josh asks, and sings, "You common hoes, you common hoe oh ohs!"

We laugh and Bobby grins. "Because that's what it *says*." He looks at me and says, "It's crazy how detailed your dream is."

"It is," I agree. "I remember a scratch on Josh's arm, what flavor of Bubblicious Caleb was chomping on … but I wanted to make sure this next part was something real, not just a dream, because it's important. When we came through those gates, by the little kid side and the petting zoo, one of the costumed employees stopped to talk to Lizzy and slapped a bracelet on her wrist. He told her he liked her shoes. Do any of you remember that?"

"I think I do," Josh says. "He was a scarecrow or something."

Bobby gives him a sharp look and Josh sighs. "Not *that* scarecrow. He wasn't scary." He scrunches his face in concentration. "Or maybe he was a clown? I remember bright, red yarn hair and overalls."

"Was it Raggedy Andy?" I ask, and Josh says, "Who the hell is Raggedy Andy?"

Caleb does a Google image search and hands his phone to Josh.

"Yeah! That's him. Why?"

"The police never interviewed a Raggedy Andy. I needed to know he existed."

"I remember him," Josh says. "He spoke in some weird voice, didn't he?"

"Yes!" I almost sob in relief. "High-pitched, like Mickey

Mouse. After that, we went to throw darts, and Bobby, you won Lizzy this ugly E.T. doll. You told her you loved her better than watermelon and she said she loved you better than ice cream."

Bobby closes his eyes. "That happened, didn't it? I'd forgotten. You don't know how many nights I've lain awake, wondering when was the last time I told her I loved her."

"She knew," I say. "We all knew. But you did tell her that night. That's why I wanted to talk about this." I shake the notepad. "Does anyone dispute any of this?"

"Cath," Bobby says patiently. "Whether the police interviewed that worker or not, that doesn't change the fact that Harton—"

Someone raps on the door.

"Hey, Mrs. Bryant, it's me!" Daniel calls.

I freeze, staring at Bobby. I don't want him to find out about Daniel like this.

"Just a minute!" I call and jump up, but Bobby is quicker. Not taking his eyes off me, he moves toward the door.

"Bobby, stop!"

He shoots me a puzzled look as he reaches for the knob.

"I've been working with someone, and that's him, but I need to warn you—"

Bobby throws open the door and the sight of Daniel leaves him thunderstruck.

BOBBY TURNS SO PALE THAT, at first, I am afraid he will have another heart attack. Then, I'm afraid he'll hurt Daniel.

"Catherine, what the hell is this?" Bobby demands in a shaky voice.

"This is Daniel ..." I pause, omitting the obvious.

Fury paints red swaths on Bobby's cheeks. Hatred burns in his eyes.

"Bobby, you don't know this boy," I plead. "He wasn't even born when Lizzy was taken."

"When his father took her!" Bobby shouts and Corey moves between them, placing his hands on his father's chest.

Daniel looks terrified.

"Mrs. Bryant, I'm so sorry!" he says. "I'll go."

"Yeah," Bobby growls. "*Go!*"

"Don't go, Daniel," I order, then, "Bobby, please. He's just like us. He doesn't know. He wants answers. For me, can you just listen to what he has to say?"

Bobby's lips press in a thin line, then he angrily motions Daniel inside. He's so focused on Daniel's face that I don't think he even notices the arm braces until Daniel walks past him to sit in the chair Corey had vacated. Bobby's face softens, but when he looks at me, his eyes are stark with pain. I feel his tension, his volatility. I know I don't have much time, so I plunge right in.

"Sheriff Anderson was Daniel's maternal grandfather. You know the sexual offense the sheriff told us Will Harton had? It was a consensual relationship with the sheriff's own daughter. She was two months shy of her 17th birthday and Will

Harton had just turned 18. That's the real reason the charges didn't stick."

"And you know this, why, because he told you?" Bobby demands. "Cath, he could tell you anything. Have you talked to the sheriff, or his daughter?"

"Both dead," I admit. "But she made a video statement. Daniel has that, and so much more."

Hurriedly, I tell them everything. Daniel lets me do the talking, occasionally nodding in confirmation.

"Did you ask them about Larry Brown?" Daniel says, when I finished.

"Who's Larry Brown?" Bobby asks with annoyance.

"He's a witness who told the police he saw Lizzy talking to a scarecrow and following him into the maze."

"That's not what they told us," Bobby says. "They told us he grabbed her and ran into the maze. I don't know where you're getting your information—"

"That's from the police files," I tell him. "Sheriff Alvarez showed us what they have, which is pitiful, but it was in there. And Will Harton passed the questions on the polygraph about Lizzy."

"She's going to try to find Larry Brown and re-interview him," Daniel says. "Mrs. Bryant said Lizzy would never have walked into the maze with him. What do you think?"

Bobby gives him a long look, then he rubs his hand over his face.

"I can't do this," he tells Daniel. "I can't look at you, and talk about her. "

Turning to me, he says, "I'm sorry, Catherine. I'll call you later, but right now, I need some air."

He stalks out the door and both Corey and Caleb take off after him. I wonder if I should, too.

Reading my thoughts, Josh says, "Just let him go. He'll be back around when he's ready." He exhales. "You realize that if you're right, you're taking the one thing from him that's kept him sane? Knowing that Lizzy's killer is dead. But yeah, if the man was innocent, we need to find out who did it. I remember Raggedy Andy." He glances at Daniel. "I also remember seeing your father walk by Lizzy and how she reacted. I remember how skittish she was."

"She wouldn't have gone into the maze with him," I say, and Josh nods.

"Not even if he had a puppy under each arm. She would've run straight to Dad as soon as he spoke to her."

"We need to find Larry Brown," Daniel says.

"I have an idea where to start," Josh says. "Steph's sister works in the clerk's office. I'll get her to run him through the computer." Then he looks at me. "I'm going to check on the old man, okay? Then I'll call my sister-in-law. I don't know if she can access the database on the weekend or not, but I'll be back in a little while either way."

"Josh," I say, as he's leaving. "I need you to go by the police station and get my car keys."

His eyes narrow. "What? Why?"

"I got a little confused last night and went to our old house instead of here. I promised the sheriff I wouldn't drive anymore."

I gloss over it, hoping the sheriff won't elaborate, but it doesn't really matter. I know they'd all be watching me now, especially my firstborn. The sadness on his face breaks my heart.

Josh hugs me tight. "I want you to move in with me and Steph. Pack a few things and I'll be back tonight to get you."

"No, Josh. I'm not going to do that. I won't be a burden to you or your family."

"Mom!" he says, his dark eyes shining. "You *are* my family."

"Please, let me be independent as long as I can be," I beg. "Give me that dignity."

He makes me promise to think about it, although I know I can't entertain the idea. Last night showed me-I was a risk not only to myself, but others. I won't put my family in harm's way.

Guiltily, I steal a glance at the scratch on Daniel's throat. I wonder if he's noticed it, and what he thinks caused it.

After Josh leaves, Daniel says, "Mrs. Bryant, I'm so sorry. I'd have never interrupted, but I thought of a way to find out about Raggedy Andy and I knew you'd want to come along. I still know Helen Parson, who worked in the petting zoo. She owns the Slick Pig restaurant in town. I thought we could go talk to her. "

THE GIRL at the register tells us that Helen is out, but she'll be back in a few minutes if we don't mind waiting.

"I'm getting a little hungry," Daniel says. "Have you eaten?"

"Not since the pizza," I admit, and my stomach rumbles. "It smells delicious," I add, glancing toward the open kitchen.

"Best barbeque in the county," the girl replies, handing us a couple of menus and leading us to a corner booth.

The barbeque tastes as good as it smells, but—hungry as I am—I'm too wired to eat much.

"Is everything okay?" the waitress asks, refilling our waters.

"It's great," I assure her, ignoring the dubious glance she casts at my plate. I smile at her and pick at the barbeque nachos while Daniel eats and searches his phone for Larry Brown from Pelham.

"Nothing," he says finally. "I hope your son has better luck."

He spears a chunk of potato salad with his fork and says, "Okay, so you and Josh both say she wouldn't have willingly gone with my father, no matter what he said, right?"

I think about it again. My answer is still the same.

"No."

"If we're to believe your dream is 100% accurate, she walked to someone. Do you think she would've gone with Raggedy Andy?"

I hesitate. "My gut impulse is no, but he'd been friendly to her. He'd given her a bracelet and he talked in that damned high-pitched voice. She might not have considered him a threat. If she really did go willingly with her kidnapper, I think this person was either Raggedy Andy or someone she knew."

Daniel mulls it over. "I'm sure the police didn't investigate that angle. As far as they were concerned, they had their man. But can you think of anyone in your day-to-day life, teachers, neighbors, coworkers, friends ... even family ... who might have taken her?"

I push my plate away. "Even though the sheriff told me he was sure your father did it, I went through this phase where I was suspicious of everyone—the mailman, the paperboy, even the old man who owned the gas station in town who always told Lizzy what a pretty little girl she was. But we'd decided to go to the maze on the spur of the moment, so no one could've known we would be there and that they'd even have an opportunity to get Lizzy alone. She usually stuck right to us and it surprises me that she would willingly walk to anyone like that, even if she knew them. So, I don't know what to think."

"Hey," the waitress says, laying the check facedown on the table. Daniel grabs it before I can. "Helen's here. She said you can come back to her office whenever you finish eating. Do you guys need to-go boxes?"

I look at Daniel and he shakes his head.

"No, thank you," I reply.

Daniel pays in cash and gives her a generous tip, earning a bright smile.

"Follow me," she says, and leads us past the restrooms to a neatly kept office in the back. A slim, dark-haired woman in a Bonnaroo shirt smiles and stands to greet us.

"Hi, Daniel!" Helen says , then she turns her gaze to me.

"Mrs. Parson," Daniel says. "This is Catherine Bryant."

Extending her hand, she says, "Mrs. Bryant. I'm so sorry for ..." She hesitates. I know she doesn't want to say *for your loss*, because Lizzy's body has never been found, but it is a truth all of us know, whether it is spoken or not.

"Thank you," I say and shake her hand. When I release it, she motions us toward the empty chairs across from her. "Please. Sit."

She looks at us with a mixture of sympathy and curiosity. We are an odd pair, I admit.

"Daniel said you had questions about that night," she says. "Honestly, I'm not sure how much I remember from back then. I was sixteen and I don't recall seeing anything unusual. I spoke to Will when I first got there, but I don't even think I saw him after I went to my station."

"We want to ask you about a worker," Daniel says. "Do you remember who dressed as Raggedy Andy? I think he worked in your area."

Helen rolls her eyes. "That was old man McDowell, Smilin' Sam himself. I always thought it was creepy as hell, how he'd speak in that weird voice, but the kids seemed to love it."

I sit frozen, unable to breathe.

"Sam McDowell was one of those guys who acted all nice in public, but not so much at home, you know? My brother was friends with his son, Walter. I was a couple of years younger, but sometimes I'd tag along when he went to the McDowell's. We'd have to sneak in most of the time, because Walter was always grounded for some reason or another." She shakes her head. "Mr. McDowell was a mean drunk."

Daniel and I share a glance and Helen continues, "At first, it was kinda hard to believe, because Mr. McDowell was always so syrupy sweet to us. But one day, I saw it for myself. They had this root cellar beneath the laundry room of his old house—not the one where they live now, " she adds quickly. "The one that burned. Anyway, it was just this little 8x8 room, accessed through a trap door in the floor. They didn't really use it for anything, and Walter said he'd hide there when his dad got really bad. We were down there smoking pot one day, and I guess we didn't close the opening well enough, because he found us and made us climb out. Sam was screaming at Walter, and he punched him right in the face. He yelled at us, too, telling us to go home before he called the police. We did, but I felt guilty for leaving Walter there. It was the weirdest thing, though. The next time I saw old man McDowell, he was all nice again. I don't think he remembered a thing."

"So, is Sam still alive?" Daniel asks.

She leans back, studying us. "Last I heard. Not in the best of health, but I guess he has to be in his mid-eighties now."

"Where do they live?" Daniel asks, and I am glad he's carrying the conversation. Was Smilin' Sam my daughter's killer? Is that what that wretched cartoon mascot has been trying to tell me all along?

"That big, fancy brick house above the corn maze. When the old one burned, they just moved it up there, away from the road."

We fall silent and then Daniel says, "Anything else you want to ask her, Mrs. Bryant?"

My thoughts are jumbled hellfire, burning and chaotic. I feel sick. I feel like I am still missing something.

"No, I don't think so," I manage. "Thank you, Mrs. Parson."

When we step out of the office, I see the restroom sign and squeeze Daniel's arm. "I need a moment."

"Yeah, take all the time you need. I'll wait for you by the counter."

I SLIP into the restroom and stand in front of the mirror, clutching the sink. Turning on the faucet, I bend to splash my face with cold water. When I raise back up, Smilin' Sam is grinning at me from *inside* the mirror. His hand comes out of the glass, giving me a little wave.

I gasp, and jerk backwards, crashing into a stall door. It flies inward and I tumble with it, falling across the toilet and smacking my head painfully against the wall.

Sam climbs out of the mirror and peers at me through the door as I weakly sit on the toilet . "Wow, you're really clumsy. Not sure how you managed to live all these years."

I touch the back of my head. It's bleeding, but not badly. I have a nice knot rising, though.

"Was it you?" I whisper. "Were you the killer all along?"

This amuses Sam. He doubles over laughing, slapping at his knee. "I don't even exist, silly. I'm just a figment of that diseased little cantaloupe you've got up there. Me, a killer. Wow. Old man McDowell, on the other hand ... eh, maybe? But even after all I've tried to show you, you still don't pay attention. You still don't ask the right questions. What is the one thing you want more than anything?"

"To find Elizabeth," I say, pushing to my feet.

"So why are you asking who, when I've given you everything you need to find out where? Do I have to draw you a fucking map, Kit-Kat?"

Suddenly, it dawns on me. "No," I whisper.

"Atta, girl," Sam says, almost fondly, then pushes into the stall with me. He hops into the toilet bowl, grabbing the handle to flush himself as he falls. He whoops and hollers as he circles the bowl, then disappears.

I grab my phone out of my pocket. My hands are shaking so badly that I can barely find Bobby's number, but I press his contact. The phone rings once and goes to voicemail.

"Meet me at the corn maze," I tell him. "I know where she is."

I start to call 9-1-1, too, but I hesitate.

What if I'm wrong?

Sheriff Alvarez already has ample reason to think I'm crazy. As I try to put the phone back into my shirt pocket, I miss and it bounces off my leg into the toilet bowl.

"No!" I cry, and fish it out. The screen lights up, but the picture glitches and disappears.

I shove it into my back pocket and hurry outside to Daniel, who is talking to the girl at the register.

He blinks at me when I stumble into the dining area. "Mrs. Bryant, are you okay?"

"Take me to Sam McDowell's."

✦

"MAYBE WE SHOULD CALL THE SHERIFF," Daniel suggests. "Get her to meet us there."

"No!" I say. "I want to talk to him first, without her. I want to see his face when I say Lizzy's name. I think I'll know. And then we can call her in. If we show up at his door with the cops, he'll just send us away and call his lawyer. Besides, after what I did last night, she'll never believe me."

The way Daniel is looking at me gives me a sinking feeling. "You don't believe me, either, do you?"

He hesitates a second before answering. "I mean, I *want* to believe you, and it sort of makes sense. I can see how someone would've called him a scarecrow if they'd just seen the Raggedy Andy face makeup and my dad's coat and hat. I also get that Lizzy might've been more likely to approach him than my father. I just can't figure out the timing. He was in the petting zoo and just happened to know when my father left his post, then he just happened to go in the maze and put on the coat and hat, then just happened to catch Lizzy ... I don't know what to think, but I definitely agree it's worth checking out."

"Maybe he followed us from the petting zoo," I say, though the thought of someone stalking her like prey threatens to bring up what nachos I'd managed to eat.

The gray October sky promises rain. Both it and my thoughts grow darker as we travel down highway 50. The billboard is still up.

It is faded now, peeling, but the scarecrow is somehow brighter than the background and lettering. It may be my imagination, but his smile seems more sinister. His dark eyes gleam with anticipation.

The field is overgrown, but I can still see the ramshackle remains of the ticket booth through the gate. Daniel doesn't turn into the parking lot, though, choosing instead the road before it that leads to the looming brick estate on the hill.

A Mercedes sits in the drive. Daniel pulls in beside it. As he puts the van in park, he raises his eyebrows and forces a smile.

"Ready, Kit-Kat?" he asks, and I blink.

"What?"

His smile falters. "Ready?"

I stare at him for a moment, then nod. I feel weak, disoriented, but determined. Today, I'm going to find answers.

Together, we shuffle up the walkway, the old woman and the disabled man. The missing child's mother and the murderer's son. What a pair we are.

I glance at the billboard again, bracing myself for Smilin' Sam's leer—

But he is gone.

Only the outline of him beside the faded, peeling paint of the cartoon corn stalks remains, and the words

SMILIN' SAM'S CORN MAZE

5 ACRES OF FAMILY FUN!

My heart beats against my ribcage, but I try to tell myself it doesn't matter. The cartoon scarecrow isn't real, and he can't hurt me. The real Smilin' Sam can't hurt me, either. He is an old man now, older than myself.

And fear not them which kill the body, but are not able to kill the soul: but rather fear him which is able to destroy both soul and body in hell.

The snatch of scripture comes unbidden, though I haven't attended church in years. I feel like Lizzy's killer has done both to me, killed my body and soul. Surely there is no greater hell than the not-knowing. The-not knowing is the only thing I fear now.

I climb the steps and ring the doorbell.

The man who answers looks younger than I expect, catching me off-guard. He regards me with quizzical dark eyes. He has a mop of curly, brown hair that looks recently dyed and unnaturally uniform in color for a man who has to be in his late fifties.

"Yes, Ma'am," he says, smiling. "Can I help—holy shit!" he says, looking past me at Daniel. He gapes at him for a moment, then he laughs.

"Wow, you don't have to tell me who you are. You've gotta be Will Harton's kid. I used to know your dad. We went to school together."

"Walter McDowell?" Daniel asks.

"Yeah! Hey," Walter offers his hand, but awkwardly withdraws it when he notices the forearm crutches Daniel wears.

He makes an effort to turn his gaze back to me. "Is this your mother?"

"Catherine Bryant," I say, and he blinks. "I'm Elizabeth Bryant's moth—"

"Wow," he interrupts, glancing from me to Daniel. "Holy shit!"

Then he shakes his head and says, "Forgive my manners, and my language, but you are about the last two people I expected to show up on my doorstep. Won't you come in?"

He swings open the door, and hesitantly, I enter, with Daniel trailing behind me.

The entryway and the living room beyond are enormous and tastefully decorated, but my eyes lock on one black-and-white picture near the coat rack—a man in a Raggedy Andy costume stooping to hand a lollipop to a grinning toddler.

Walter catches my gaze. "My father. Old Smilin' Sam himself."

"Is he here?" I ask. "Can we speak with him?"

Walter gives an apologetic sigh. "My father ... he's very ill."

"It won't take long," I plead. "I just have a few questions."

He opens his mouth, then shuts it again. He starts down the hall, motioning for Daniel and I to follow. We share a cautious glance, then trail behind him.

The room beside the living room had perhaps once been a dining room or a family room, but it has been converted to a hospital room. A frail old man lies in a hospital bed, hooked up to a myriad of beeping, whirring machines. He is nearly as colorless as his sheets. If the machines weren't telling us he was alive, I would doubt it.

"He hasn't spoken in nearly a month," Walter says, dropping his gaze. "But you're welcome to try."

I see the hesitation in Daniel's eyes, but I'm desperate. I approach the bed.

"Mr. McDowell?" I say softly. "Smilin' Sam?"

No movement. Nothing but the hiss of his oxygen.

"My name is Catherine Bryant. My little girl, Lizzy, went missing in the maze in 1984."

I stare down at his liver-spotted hand. Had he ever raised this hand to my daughter?"

Suddenly, I am furious. He has lived his entire life, nearly a century, and Lizzy only had seven years. It wasn't fair. It has never been fair.

I stare at that claw-like hand with its yellowed nails, then force myself to take it. It feels limp and birdlike in mine and I want to crush it, to cause him some measure of pain for all the pain he's caused us. Some small retribution for the pain he'd surely caused *her*.

"Mr. McDowell—*Sam*—I'd like to ask you about Lizzy. Can you hear me?"

No response, not the slightest change on the little blips that measured his heartbeat. Bitterness scalds me and I blink back tears. I feel lost. I feel *devastated*.

Focus, Kit-Kat, Smilin' Sam's voice inside my head says with unusual patience. *It's not the who, it's the—*

"Where," I whisper, and release the old man's hand. Turning to Walter, I say, "We've been looking into the case again, Daniel and I. We were told there was an old root cellar on the property. Do you know if it's still there, and if the police ever searched it?

Walter blinks at me, then purses his mouth and looks up, thinking. "I really couldn't say, Mrs. Bryant. I feel like my father might have had it filled in after the fire, but I can't say for sure. That was a long, long time ago. Before the maze was even built."

"Do you mind if we look?" Daniel asks.

"No," Walter says immediately. "Of course not. I can show you where the old foundation was. I just don't want to leave my father too long."

"Of course," Daniel says. "We understand."

We follow him outside of the room. I cast one last glance at Smilin' Sam. If I could torture him, wring the information out of him in any way possible, I am capable of it. But he is just a shell of a person lying there. Much like I will soon be a shell of the person I used to be lying in a hospital bed.

"Thatta girl," a familiar voice whispers, and I see the cartoon scarecrow peeking at me through the banister as Walter fetches his shoes.

What are you doing here? I thought, glaring at him, and Sam merely smiles.

Oh, Kit-Kat ... I wouldn't miss this for the world.

"Can you two walk?" Walter asks. "There's another road, on the other side that was the old driveway, but it's not been used or kept up. It's fine for walking, but I don't know if I'd take a vehicle on it. It's not very far. Really close to the billboard."

"I can manage," Daniel says, and I nod.

"Me, too."

Walter gives us a dubious glance, but he nods and walks into the kitchen, pausing to grab a flashlight from a drawer.

"Have you told anyone about this?" he asks. "The police or anyone?"

I'd forgotten all about my frantic call to Bobby until then, but before I can answer, Daniel says, "No. We just heard about it."

Walter frowns. "If you two don't mind, I think I'd like to call the sheriff, get someone out here with us. Liability issues, I'm sure you understand." He pats his paunch and chuckles, "Surely they have someone more capable than any of us of crawling down that hole, assuming it wasn't filled in."

He squints at his phone, scrolling through his contacts.

"Non-emergency number," he explains to us, then, "Hi! This is Walter McDowell, at 27102 State Route 50. Can I speak to the sheriff? Yes, I'll hold." He gives us a patient smile and I look at Daniel. Sheriff Alvarez probably won't be happy to see us again so soon, but I'm glad Walter is calling her.

He briefs the sheriff on what we are doing and assures her that, yes, we'll wait for an officer before we do anything other than locate the root cellar.

"C'mon," Walter says. "We'll go out the back. Closer this way and I'll grab a shovel from the shed."

He disappears into the building for a moment, then emerges, handing me the flashlight as he props the shovel on his shoulder. The three of us make our way down a thin, snaking gravel road. Well, four of us, if you count Sam, who is whistling and skipping ahead of us. I make a concentrated effort not to acknowledge him.

"Who told you about the root cellar?" Walter asks. "There can't have been many people who would've known about it. Even I'd forgotten it."

"Helen Parson," Daniel says. "We were just talking and she mentioned how y'all used to smoke in there."

Walter laughs. "Ah, Helen. How is she? I don't get out much these days. I need to stop by and catch up."

They chat, but my stomach churns and I can't force myself to participate. Occasionally, Sam turns to grin at me, but I ignore him, too.

Please, let me find her, I pray.

"The sheriff should be here soon," Walter says. "He said he'd come himself."

I shoot Daniel a sharp look, but Walter doesn't seem to notice. Daniel doesn't seem to notice, either, so I wonder if I'd misheard, but then again, Daniel has fallen behind us a bit, navigating a particularly tricky patch of road with his crutches. I open my mouth to ask Walter, '*What do you mean, he?*' but Sam puts his finger to his lips and hisses, "Shhh!"

"This used to be the employee parking area," Walter says, pointing. "The restrooms were there, the ticket counter there ... all the games were over that way. the maze was over here ... I guess you know all of that, though." He coughs, then says, "The old home foundation was behind the maze. You can still see some of the cinder blocks in the ground.

An icy finger traces my spine and I drop my head. Something is wrong. Something is—

"It's really wild how much you look like your dad," Walter tells Daniel. "Like seeing a ghost. Genetics are so crazy sometimes. My dad and I, we never looked anything alike. He had reddish blonde hair when he was young, and blue eyes. I took after my mom."

My head snaps up and I turn to look straight into those dark eyes of his. If I remember anything about Raggedy Andy from those dreams, it is those shiny, black eyes.

"Oooooh!" Smilin' Sam shrieks behind me. "Now we're getting to the good stuff!"

My expression stops Walter in his tracks.. Then he smirks and tosses the shovel aside. Before I can react, he pulls a gun from his jacket pocket and points it at my face.

"What are you doing?" Daniel shouts.

Walter ignores him.

"She cried for you, you know," he tells me, then he laughs.

I glance at Daniel, who is white as a sheet.

"Y'all have just ... blown my mind!" Walter continues, shaking his head. "Of all people to show up at my door!" To Daniel, he says, "Sorry about your dad. I liked him. My father made me work the maze sometimes in his place. Most of the workers avoided me, because they thought I was him in that get-up, especially when I talked in that stupid voice."

"Hey!" Smilin' Sam exclaims indignantly from behind me.

"Why did you frame my dad?" Daniel asks, trying to put himself between me and Walter, but Walter motions him back.

"That was kind of an accident, really. I followed Lizzy

from the petting zoo, just watching. Man, she was so pretty. So sweet. Cute as a damn bug! I was standing around outside the maze when Kelly Jones bumped into me and asked me to go tell Will his girlfriend needed him in the employee parking lot. I went to get him and he took off, leaving his coat and hat. I was just fooling around when I tried it on and walked out of the maze, thinking it would be cool to work in the scary part sometime." He glances at me. "I was just hanging out, watching, waiting on Will to come back. That's when I saw you and your son, running toward the restroom, and sweet little Lizzy trailing behind. I'd heard your boys teasing her about how they were going to race in the maze. So, I said, 'Hey, Lizzy! I know a shortcut. I'll show you how to beat your brothers!" He shrugs. "And that was that. Easy Peasy, Lemon Squeezy."

"Why did you take her?" I choke, and he just gives me that sly smile again. "Oh, Catherine—can I call you that? Don't make me say it. You know why."

I don't see it coming, and Walter certainly doesn't, either. The shovel smacks the side of Walter's face so hard it knocks him off his feet. He goes sprawling, grunting, into the gravel.

Bobby stands there, his face stricken, his eyes burning with fury.

"Oooh, ooh! Get him, Daddy-O!" Smilin' Sam screams, "Hit him again!"

And Bobby does.

Walter shrieks and paws at the ground beside him.

"Bobby, the gun!" I shout.

Bobby stomps his wrist so hard I think I hear it snap. He straddles Walter, positioning the shovel blade at his throat.

"Okay!" Walter yells. "Okay, I give!"

When Bobby doesn't move, Walter pleads. "Think this over. I'm unarmed. If you kill me, you'll go to prison for the rest of your life."

Bobby sneers. "I'm 71-years-old! Like I give a fuck."

The cartoon scarecrow who plagues my nightmares lies on his stomach, on the ground beside them like a referee. He slaps the earth and yells, "Finish him! Finish him!"

I don't know what Walter sees in Bobby's face, but he stops pleading. He smiles.

"She cried for you, too," he says. "But you didn't even know she was gone. You were too busy playing with toy guns. *Pew pew*!"

"Finish him!" Smilin' Sam roars in a deep, demonic voice.

Bobby raises the shovel above his head and brings it down with all his might, decapitating Walter.

Blood spurts from his neck, a river of blood, and his head rolls to a stop by my feet. His dark eyes shine in the moonlight like new buttons and he still wears a ferocious grin.

"Cathi!" Bobby gasps, and clutches his chest. Then he collapses.

"No!" I shout, nearly falling over Walter's corpse to get to him.

Dimly, I hear Daniel call 9-1-1, but Bobby isn't breathing and I can't stop screaming.

I SIT in the waiting room with my kids, their spouses and Bobby's girlfriend, Ashley. The doctor comes out to tell us he's made it through surgery and he's awake, but he's weak.

"He's asking for his wife," the nurse says.

Ashley looks at me, then jumps to her feet and hurries into the recovery room. I am too exhausted to argue with her.

Apparently, Bobby isn't, because she comes back out as quickly as she ran in.

"He must be delirious," she snaps. "He's asking for you."

Josh helps me to my feet, then keeps his arm around me as he guides me to the curtained off room where Bobby lies. Corey, Caleb and Ashley fall in behind us. I expect the nurse to protest, but it seems we are the only ones back here. Bobby lies back against the pillows, his pale face anxious.

"Did they find her?" he asks, reaching for me.

I slip away from Josh and cross to take Bobby's big, rough hand in mine. "I don't know," I say. "I jumped in the ambulance with you. I messed up my phone, so I haven't talked to Daniel, either."

Tears well in his blue eyes. "Cath, I'm sorry. I lost it. I shouldn't have—"

"Shhh, no!" I say, squeezing his fingers. "I'm glad he's dead. No matter what they find or don't find, I'm glad he's dead."

"What happened?" Bobby asks. "How did you figure it out?"

I give them an abbreviated version. Even without the Smilin' Sam stuff, I know it sounds crazy.

"I got that message from you, so I just drove to the maze. I was trying to call you back when I saw the three of you walking down the hill and something told me to hang back. I'm glad I did."

"If you hadn't, we would all be dead," I say.

Sheriff Alvarez knocks on the wall, announcing herself. "Mrs. Bryant, can I see you out here for a moment?"

Bobby grips my hand and asks, "Did you find her?"

Sheriff Alvarez shoots a reluctant glance at his heart monitor and Bobby says, "Look, you're stressing me out more by *not* telling me."

She sighs and says, "We found the root cellar and what appears to be the remains of a child. We'll have to do some testing to be sure, but given the description of her clothing, we believe it's Elizabeth."

"Oh, thank God!" I whisper, feeling hot tears spill down my cheeks. Bobby's hand grips mine, and I bend to kiss his knuckles.

"You brought our baby home, Cath," he says softly, and we smile at each other.

The sheriff looks away, her eyes suddenly shiny. When she speaks, her tone is gruff. "Daniel said it was self-defense, that McDowell was going to shoot you and you had no recourse. I've already spoken to the D.A. and he assures me that he has no desire to bring charges against you, especially considering the fact that, upon searching the house, we have reason to believe that your daughter might not have been his only victim. I'll need to get a statement from both of you, just for the file, but that can wait for now. Get well soon, Mr. Bryant."

We watch her leave and I say, "Daniel called 9-1-1 and told me how to do CPR on you until the ambulance got there. When you collapsed, I was a complete mess. I don't know what I'd have done without him."

"Tell him I said thank you," Bobby says. "For everything. And that I'm sorry." He looks around at each of us, his gaze lingering on Ashley when he says, "Ashley, I don't want to hurt you, but while we're all here, I want to make something clear. When I die, I want to be buried in Payne's Cove, with Catherine and with Elizabeth. Where I belong."

Ashley's mouth sets in a grim line and she says, "Why wait? Y'all can be together right now! Have one of your kids pick up your stuff. It'll be on the porch."

Then she storms from the room.

"Kids ..." Josh jokes, and the boys laugh. Bobby gives me a sheepish grin and says, "Got room on your couch, darlin'?"

I smile and brush a strand of his too-long hair from his forehead. "I've always got room for you."

They let one of us stay with him and I insist it's me, despite the boys' worries.

"I'm fine," I assure them. "Your father and I have a lot to talk about."

After extracting promises from both of us to call if we need anything, they leave.

"Get over here, gal," Bobby says, and scoots over to make room for me in his bed. I figure his nurses will say something, but Bobby is something of a local hero now. The night nurse just smiles and says, "Easy, tiger. Don't get that heart rate up too much."

I lie nestled in his arms for the first time in decades. We are both too wired to sleep, so we talk about the kids, the grand-kids ... everything. It feels good to hold him. To laugh. I can't help but think that this is a glimpse of the life that had been taken from us. It is the way things should have always been.

"I'm sorry, Catherine. For every time I let you down. For every time I failed you."

"You never failed me," I say. "Like today. When I needed you, you came through."

He kisses the top of my head and says, "I love you, Cath. Always have, always will."

"I love you, too, Bobby Bryant," I say, and fall asleep.

I OPEN my eyes in the hallway of our old house. Soft music plays from the end of the hallway and I wander toward it, trailing my fingers on the wallpaper.

Bobby stands in front of the big mirror in our bedroom, adjusting his tie and straightening his gray suit. He is young again, so strong and tanned. I just stand back for a moment and watch him, as smitten as I've ever been at the sight of him. His blue eyes twinkle and he smiles when I slip up behind him and wrap my arms around his waist.

"Well, don't you look handsome!" I say, tiptoeing to put my chin on his shoulder and stare at our reflections. I am young again, too, but not dressed nearly as nicely as he is. "Big date?"

He laughs. "Yup! It's where she wants to go."

Before I can ask who he means, I hear the clack-clack of shoes running down the hall and Elizabeth bursts into the room. When I see the cornflower blue dress she wears, I know.

The Father-Daughter dance at her elementary school. She'd been so excited about it—had planned for it since that August—but had never gotten to attend, as it was to be held the first weekend in November.

"Mama!" she says, and runs to me.

I scoop her up and hold her to me. It feels so real. *She* feels so real. I can smell her hair, feel the warmth of her little body and the stiffness of her dress. She lets me hold her for a long moment, then she begins to wriggle. Reluctantly, I set her down.

"Come on, Daddy!" she cries, grabbing his hand. "We can't be late."

"Alright, alright!" he says, shooting me a grin as he allows her to tug him toward the door. "I hope you have your dancing shoes on, because we're going to show those cats how it's done."

"What cats?" she asks with a giggle. "You're silly, Daddy."

He turns and moonwalks down the hall, making us both laugh.

"Are you gonna do *that?*" she asks.

"Oh, yeah!" he says. "And the slide, and the robot, and the funky chicken ... maybe even the worm!"

Elizabeth shrieks with laughter. "No, not the *worm!* But you can do the chicken. I like the chicken."

Then they are both flapping and clapping down the

hallway and into the living room. I laugh so hard my sides hurt as I follow along behind them. They are just alike, those two. Peas in a pod.

It isn't The Beast in the driveway, but the gleaming black 1970 Cuda Bobby owned when we were seniors.

"Special car for a special date," he winks, and walks around to open the passenger door for Elizabeth.

Suddenly, a wave of sadness rolls over me and I don't want them to leave. Bobby must see it, because he pulls me into his arms and gives me a long, sweet kiss. Then he cups my face in his hands. His handsome face is suddenly anxious, pleading.

"I'll watch her, Cath. I'll take care of her," he swears, as if I have any doubt.

"I know you will," I whisper, and hug him tight.

I let him climb into the driver's seat, shut the door and start the engine. He reaches for my hand and clasps my fingers.

"See you soon," he rasps, blue eyes shining. "I'll save you a seat."

I WAKE to the sound of Bobby's heart monitor blaring. They hustle me out of the room, but I know even before they come out to tell me that he is gone. Although I grieve him to the bottom of my soul, I know he is alright. He just has other plans.

I'm deteriorating pretty quickly these days, both physically and mentally. When Daniel came to visit me yesterday, I thought he was his father again, and he had to correct me. He's doing well, and even started dating that girl from the Slick Pig —Mandy, I think her name is. He seems happy, and I'm glad.

This may be my last journal entry. I dream about Bobby and Elizabeth every day, sometimes even when I'm not sleeping. I can't wait to see them again. To hold them. But I want to make the most of these last days with my sons and grandchildren, to be present and not slip into the past, because I love them just as much.

Josh, Caleb, Corey ... if any of you read this, I love you, and I'm sorry for the times I wasn't able to be the parent you needed. After Elizabeth disappeared, it was so hard to hold the pieces of myself together. I was never whole again, but I tried. I tried so hard.

Soon, I'll be with them again. I feel the clock counting down. Maybe that's what heaven is like. Reuniting with the ones you've lost and saving seats for the ones yet to join you. You can be sure, I'll be the first one there with my arms wide open when I get to see all of you again.

Only one thing bothers me about dying, and I'm trying to push the thought away. Last week, Josh drove me across town for some tests and we passed by the corn maze. When I looked at the faded billboard, it disturbed me to see that Smilin' Sam wasn't there. Not like before, when I could see the outline of where he'd ripped himself free. There was no outline now. In his place stood faded, peeling stalks of corn, like he'd never been there. I needed to see if Josh saw it, too.

"What happened to the scarecrow?" I asked, and he frowned.

"What scarecrow?"

"The one on the sign. The cartoon scarecrow."

Josh gave me that worried look that seemed permanently etched on his face whenever he looked at me these days. "Mom, I drive by this place every day. There's never been a scarecrow on that sign."

That terrified me, more than I could admit to Josh. I try to tell myself that Smilin' Sam had *never* been real, that he's only something my brain created to organize all the clues my subconscious had captured about that night, but I know I'm lying to myself. He is more than that. Something chaotic and taunting and ... *hungry*. As my time dwindles, I have this nagging, increasing fear that he—not Bobby and Elizabeth—will be the one saving me a seat. I try to push that thought away, like I do every thought of him, but it settles in my stomach like a cold puddle of dread.

Did I create Sam? I don't think so. But I think I freed him.

God help me, I think I freed him.

About the Author

You can follow Stephanie at www.facebook.com/stephaniescissom2019.

Made in the USA
Columbia, SC
03 June 2024